D0466935

Animal
Survivors

Written by Clive Gifford

Illustrated by Sarah Horne

EGMONT
We bring stories to life

Book Band: Gold

Adapted from *Dead or Alive?* first published in Great Britain 2014

Animal Survivors first published in Great Britain 2017
by Red Shed, an imprint of Egmont UK Limited
The Yellow Building, 1 Nicholas Road, London W11 4AN

www.egmont.co.uk

Text copyright © Egmont UK Limited 2014, 2017
Illustrations copyright © Sarah Horne 2014, 2017

ISBN 978 1 4052 8492 9

A CIP catalogue record for this book is available from The British Library.

Printed in Singapore
65791/1

Series and book banding consultant: Nikki Gamble

Animal Survivors

Reading Ladder

Contents

Introduction

Every day, millions of animals fight for survival. Most are simply trying to avoid being eaten. Some are desperate to find food or water. Others need to shelter from extreme cold or heat.

Many of these creatures have developed amazing ways to save themselves. Read on to find out how they live – or die!

Playing dead

A brilliant way to outwit a hunter is to fake death. Many predators only like to eat animals that they kill themselves. This is to stop them getting ill from eating rotting meat.

Cheetah

Antelope

In Africa, antelopes would not be fast enough to escape a cheetah if they made a run for it. So some antelopes play dead, because the cheetah likes fresh meat.

When threatened, an opossum falls onto its side, goes rigid and drools from its snout. It can stay like this for up to four hours to escape being eaten!

Opossum

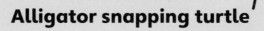

Alligator snapping turtle

Setting a trap

Animals need to eat to survive. The alligator snapping turtle gets its food by staying very, very still. It lies in the water with its giant jaws wide open, looking like a rocky cave.

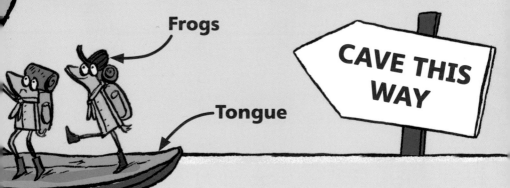

Frogs

Tongue

CAVE THIS WAY

The turtle's tongue looks just like a juicy worm. Fish, frogs and other river creatures are tempted in, but the deadly jaws snap shut!

Brief lives

Some creatures live for just a few years, months or days.

An adult mayfly's mouthparts are just for show. They live less than a day – not long enough to get hungry!

Mayflies

Gastrotrichs go from eggs to dead in three days.

Gastrotrichs

As nymphs, dragonflies live underwater for up to five years. Then they become flying adults that live for four months.

Dragonflies

Labord's chameleon

Labord's chameleon only has four months to grow and mate before it dies.

2
MONTHS
OLD
TODAY

Long-living legends

Some animals survive anything and everything to reach a ripe old age!

Some giant tortoises live for hundreds of years. A Galapagos tortoise, discovered by scientist Charles Darwin in 1835, lived until she was 175 years old.

Galapagos tortoise

Ocean quahogs, a type of clam, have yearly growth rings, so it is easy to tell how old they are. One lived for more than 500 years!

Ocean quahog

Bowhead whales can live for more than 200 years. They may be the longest-living mammals on Earth.

Bowhead whale

Pet survival

Pets are amazing – some more so than others! These pets have death-defying stories to tell.

Sophie, an Australian cattle dog, was washed overboard at sea. She doggy paddled eight kilometres through shark-infested waters to a desert island before being rescued!

Sugar the cat fell 60 metres from the window of a 19th-floor flat in Boston, USA. Amazingly, she did not even break a bone!

Rhino the hamster died and was buried in the garden. But the next day, this escape artist woke up and burrowed his way out!

Plucky animals

Some brave animals have looked disaster in the eye, but carried on living.

Two five-month-old pigs escaped from an English abattoir in 1998. They swam across a river and were on the run for more than a week. They were finally caught, but allowed to live their lives to the full.

In 2005, Molly the pony survived Hurricane Katrina, but when she was rescued, she was bitten by a dog and lost a leg. However, a kind surgeon made her an artificial leg, complete with hoof!

A cocker spaniel puppy was accidentally flushed down a toilet by his four-year-old owner, and got stuck. Fortunately, a drains company pulled him out safely four hours later.

17

Against all the odds

Many creatures, from tiny bacteria to giant dinosaurs, have died out. However, some animals that we thought were extinct have turned up again!

The Lord Howe Island stick insect was declared extinct in 1930. However, 71 years later, 30 were found on Ball's Pyramid in the Pacific Ocean.

Lord Howe Island stick insects

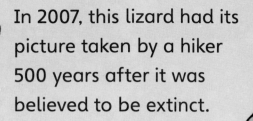

In 2007, this lizard had its picture taken by a hiker 500 years after it was believed to be extinct.

La Palma giant lizard

Coelacanth

In 1938, Captain Hendrick Goosen caught an unusual fish off the coast of South Africa. It was a coelacanth, thought to have been extinct for more than 65 million years.

Winter sleep

Some animals miss out on winter. They survive the cold and lack of food by going into an inactive state to save energy. This is called hibernation.

American black bear

Some animals use the weather or the length of sunlight in a day to decide when to hibernate. Chemicals inside their bodies may trigger them to wake up when spring comes and it gets warmer.

The American black bear can go 100 days without food, drink or going to the toilet. It can do this because it has eaten lots of nuts, berries, honey and small mammals during the summer.

Garter snakes

Many creatures hibernate alone, but garter snakes in Canada hibernate in large groups for warmth.

Summer sleep

With temperatures off the scale and a lack of food and water, some clever critters go into summer shutdown. This is called aestivation.

Water-holding frog

South American Marpesia butterflies stay above ground when they aestivate. They gather on branches in clusters of 50 or more.

Marpesia butterflies

During the rainy season in Australia, this water-holding frog gains about 50 per cent of its weight in water. It then burrows underground away from the sun and drought and aestivates for up to two years.

The frog covers itself with a moist mucus that stops it from drying out.

Frozen in time

Some amazing creatures survive the cold by letting parts of their bodies freeze. When the weather warms up, they come alive again.

In extreme cold, the wood frog freezes completely. Its heart does not beat or its kidneys work until it begins to thaw again.

Wood frog

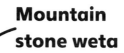

Mountain stone weta

The mountain stone weta of New Zealand can survive temperatures of below minus 10°C by freezing solid. Its brain and heart stop working until it defrosts in warm weather.

25

Ultimate survivors

Tardigrades are death-defying critters. They are short and plump and have eight stubby legs. Yet they are able to survive extremes of temperature all over Earth as well as in space.

150°C

Tardigrades can withstand temperatures as high as 150°C, or as low as minus 100°C.

A real Tardigrade (magnified 250 times)

Actual Size:
0.1 to 1.6 millimetres long.

Tardigrades have managed to survive in space outside a spacecraft without air, water, or protection from the Sun's rays.

Record breakers

There are some animal survivors that deserve an award!

Adwaita was a giant tortoise from the Seychelles. His shell was carbon dated after his death. He was between 250 and 255 years old!

Giant tortoise

Assassin bug

Spider

An assassin bug uses its legs to pluck at a spider's web. The spider thinks that prey has arrived and goes to investigate, only to be eaten itself!

When threatened, a hognose snake flattens out its head to look more fierce and deadly. If that does not work, it turns upside down with its tongue lolling out.

Hognose snake

This amazing actor also gives off a disgusting, rotting smell to put off coyotes, raccoons, foxes and hawks!

Fun facts

Giant southern darner dragonflies are fast fliers. They can zip away from predators at speeds of more than 60 kilometres an hour.

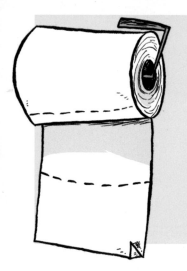

Some hibernating creatures, including certain dormice, raccoons and gophers, wake up during the winter. They take a bathroom break and eat food they stored.

One litre of water in a sea estuary can contain as many as 25,000 tardigrades!

Glossary

abattoir   A place where animals that are reared for their meat are killed.

aestivation   When a creature goes into a dormant state because of hot and dry conditions.

carbon dating   A scientific technique used to estimate the age of a once-living creature.

extinction   When a species of living thing completely dies out so that there are none of them left alive.

hibernation   When a creature goes into a dormant state because of cold conditions.

insect   A small creature with six legs and a body formed of three parts: the head, middle section (called a thorax) and the abdomen.

mammal   A type of animal, such as a mouse, cow or human. It has a backbone, is warm-blooded, usually gives birth to live young and feeds its young on milk.

nymph   The young stage in the life of many insects before they become fully grown adults.

mucus   A slimy substance that can moisten and protect an animal.

predator   A creature that hunts and feeds on other creatures

Index